I0712752

THE GREAT ADVENTURES OF MKNIK MIKO IN ARMENIA

AS CHEESY AS IT SOUNDS, IT'S OKAY TO BE DIFFERENT

Linet Gasparyan   Illustrated by Luisa Galstyan

THE GREAT ADVENTURES OF MKNIK MIKO IN ARMENIA

AS CHEESY AS IT SOUNDS, IT'S OKAY TO BE DIFFERENT

Linet Gasparyan

Illustrations by Luisa Galstyan

ISBN: 979-8-9889049-0-8

To my husband, who inspired the main character in this book named Mknik Miko; to my parents, who made up stories to put me to sleep after seeing a nightmare as a child. To my sister, who inspired me from childhood to adulthood; to my nephew and nieces, who sparked the idea of this book over a decade ago. And to Mamin, who is always in my heart and memory! Last but not least, to my beautiful daughter Mané, who changed the story of my life instantly from non-fiction to fantasy. You make everything magical!

I am forever thankful to God for all of my blessings, for all my family and friends, and for the possibility that this book may reach countless Armenian children around the world and connect them to their beautiful homeland, Armenia!

Barev! My name is Mknik Miko. I was born and live in Armenia! I love going on adventures, which is why I always carry my grandpa's magical duduk with me. And this might surprise you, but I'm a mouse who hates cheese! Oh, and if that didn't surprise you enough, my best friend is a cat! Gevo the Katu. The other mice don't like me because I hate cheese. They think I'm weird, so they never play or eat with me at lunchtime at school.

Luckily, I have my friend Gevo the Katu to go on adventures with. But our greatest adventure was unlike anything we had experienced before! It all started after our first day of school when I met Gevo the Katu at Hraparak.

ROSE'S CAFE

I told him that once again, I ate alone and was even forced to give my dolma to Rob the Mighty Mouse in class. Gevo the Katu then told me something special his grandma taught him over the summer. She said, "There's a mountain called Mount Aragats in Armenia, where many years ago, Kings and Queens would only eat one delicious cheese that was loved by everyone because it was so creamy and tasty!" Gevo the Katu said that we should go there because I would definitely love this cheese. And then, I would fit in with all the other mice and have more friends.

ABOVYAN Str.

So we decided to go on an adventure at sunrise. Our mission was to find this special cheese so I could finally be like the rest of the mice. Tomorrow, we would set out on our most magical adventure of all. "Mount Aragats, here we come!" I excitedly shouted. As the sun came up, we met at the taxi on the empty street and were ready to hit the road.

But unfortunately, it broke down next to Sevan Lake. Thankfully, I remembered that my grandpa had given me his duduk to carry with me. He told me about its magical powers, which only worked if I prayed and believed hard enough. And guess what? It worked! All of a sudden, the duduk transformed into an amazing boat!

We got in and used it to cross the river. But on the way, a big, scary, and scaly Ishkhan fish stopped the boat. And before we could do anything, it started telling us how he used to be a king, many years ago, but was transformed into a fish by an evil bird!

He went on to say that he needed to go to Noravank, a nearby church, to drink a special red juice. He said that the juice would change him back into the king and ruler of the old mountain, Mount Aragats. "That's the same mountain we're headed to. We could help you get to the church and then to the mountain if you'd like!" I replied. He was so happy and decided to come with us!

So, Tigran the Ishkhan, Gevo the Katu, and I finally reached our destination, standing in front of the beautiful Noravank church. We were amazed by how stunning it was. But suddenly, we heard a loud, thunderous noise. Tigran the Ishkhan ran inside, and we followed. It was so quiet inside Noravank, you could hear a pin drop. We entered inside, only to find a very old man dressed in all black.

At first, Gevo the Katu and I were frightened. But then Tigran the Ishkhan and the old man ran and hugged each other. The old man used to be Tigran the Ishkhan's guard when he was King of Mount Aragats. He was there on that dreadful day when Tigran was turned into a fish by the evil bird. But the old man always had faith that Tigran would come back for the magical red drink. He kept it safe in the church for hundreds of years so Tigran could return to the great, strong, fair, and kind King he always was.

The old man gave Tigran the red juice, but before taking a drink, he reminded Tigran to remember how he had felt as a king. He needed him to have faith and believe he was a king once again. And so, Tigran did as he was told and took a big sip from the cup.Our eyes couldn't believe what happened next! The entire church turned white, and we no longer saw a fish, but a tall and strong king. It was Tigran the Great! The King! After the excitement had died down, the old man warned us about the evil birds who still ruled the path to Mount Aragats. We needed to stay safe and remember that the evil birds only feared one thing - loud sounds.

We said thank you and goodbye to the old man and continued on our journey to the mountain. We walked what seemed like days as Lusine, the moon, guided us on our path through the night. After several hours, we were too tired to continue, so we fell asleep under the blanket of beautiful shining stars. As the sun rose, we awoke to see that Lusine had led us to the beginning of the trail to the top of Mount Aragats. So, we began walking. Some parts of the mountain were so steep that Gevo the Katu let me jump on his back to help me climb up the rest of the way.

We climbed and climbed for many hours until we heard some frightening sounds coming from above. We looked up and saw the evil birds the old man warned us about. They flew right toward Tigran the Great and tried to push him off the mountain! I remembered what the old man said about their fear of loud sounds. I immediately took out my grandpa's magical duduk and played his favorite Armenian melody. This instantly scared the birds and saved us.

We continued climbing until we saw the cheesy white tip of the mountain. When we arrived, there were thousands of mice, cats, and people who welcomed us with open arms as they realized their beloved king was back to rule their land. They took him to the throne where he belonged and would continue to rule and take care of his land and people.

Even throughout all the excitement, I still wondered, "Where is this magical cheese?" I asked the great king, and he replied, "Oh my friend, this isn't any cheese, this is matson. The mice here never liked cheese; they always loved to eat matson instead. So, as a gift, I covered the land with endless matson for them to enjoy eternally."I was very surprised! But I tried some matson - and it was delicious! All of the others ate with me too.

I finally felt like I fit in. I had found other mice who hated cheese but loved this delicious white dreamy food called matson. So, we ate matson, danced, and celebrated together. Not only for the return of Tigran the Great - but also because I didn't have to fit in everywhere.

I just had to be myself, and I would find the right friends for me. It was okay to be different. It led me to the greatest adventure of my life, meeting new people, finding new friends, and discovering this delicious food called matson!